Colorful Scars

Prose And Poetry

Tanya Angel

ISBN-13: 9798352176092
ISBN-10: 1477123456

Cover design by: Art Painter
Library of Congress Control Number: 2018675309
Printed in the United States of America

To John, who inspired me to write this book.

Is it really possible to tell someone else what one feels?
--LEO TOLSTOY

Contents

Preface

You are seeing my art with your eyes. My words come to you from my heart first, and then my mind. They bare my emotions, my feelings, myself. I place them before you as they come to me, somewhat reserved, somewhat coy and shy, but nevertheless genuine and true. In them you will discover my soul. Your fingers may flip through the words casually, maybe indifferently, but be aware, you are visiting me. I hope you find each word as captivating as it was meant to be. And I hope you will appreciate the meanings that lie there. Because this art is me.

Remembrances

When I had gotten to the last of them,
pictures from a box my mother kept,
of family, friends, neighbors, acquaintances,
my early life all there,
all deceased, dully mummified by her,
they told a story, chapter, and verse,
one after another, each an apothegm,
each as imperative to my life as air.

Was I ever that young? That happy?

I paused before my father, hunched and stilled
by twenty-five, twenty years more to live,
his sad gray bulk was sensing his future.
I put my finger to his face as if to turn it
to make him laugh, or to at least smile.
He did that so seldom, and needed it most.
I turn myself around and gingerly walk away,

from the past, from the brink because I know
I have things to do, things my father had as well.
Between us, he and I can do them together:
my best piece of poetry, on veracity, my best life.
And we, not just me, can find our peace.

All Is Lost

Love comes unseen; we can only see it when it goes.

—HENRY R. DOBSON

After reading the message, you set the phone down, and the whole world trembled. You trembled.

Two fireflies in the periphery glowed, and the air singed as if from a blazing fire. You felt singed.

The message delivered the news of the crash, the shock, that all perished.

All is lost.

All that was.

All that might have been.

All that will never be.

New depths of love that you might come to know—you will never know.

Lost.

That music that so enthralled her—

The things that she held so dear—

The places where she had been—

She spoke of them so lovingly that you loved them too.

Lost.

Days when you lost yourselves, are now lost too.

All you have is pictures, many, though too few.

And her seashells, many, though too few.

To hear her now, you must hold them up to your ear.

Her many worlds are at your ear, though too few.

Chatting At A Party

What is better than good advice?
It is good advice for free.
And that's what I sought at a party
from a noted psychiatrist.

"Doctor," I said, "I have a problem."
She wrinkled her nose a bit,
looked for help, and there wasn't any,
so she said, "Tell me about it."

"I'm supposed to be a poet," I said.
"All life's awfulness to be described by me.
Not happiness, which is an illusion and free,
But sorrow and grief which is grist to me."

"I've newly arrived in this state, California,
where I have yet to sadly brood.
It's been months now, and hardly a care.
Before long, I may not even remember how."

"And another problem is that my drinking is down.
I don't have a third drink, nor at time even two.
Doctor, this isn't like me; this isn't me at all.
Could it be that I may stop drinking like you?"

"Oh, I can write a happy poem, and so can you.
On love, or a poem of happiness and serenity.

But they don't sell, no matter how good they are.
No, the hurts, rubs, and harms are what sell."

"You should know, there's no substitute for tragedy!
And all the burdens and baggage that come with it.
It is on this side of life that a poet wants to be.
To show what life is like that way, to make a poet's pay."

The psychiatrist responded--

"Here is my aphorism for free: Happy people are monogamous. Even in California. So how do your poems pay? Without the paraphernalia of betrayal and hurt, jealousy and hate, eternal melancholy? That's not possible, as you learned. How do you remedy the situation?"

"First of all, I don't give a shit. Second, I hate you.
You say you don't know how to hurt or feel jealous.
In truth, you have my ex-mate, whom I name
my husband-in-law. Now isn't that funny?"

"So you may laugh about what Cyril Connolly
has called the contrite confusion of marriage.
Which may be the best part, though without
the morality and menace which make for fine art."

"Of course, it won't last. It hardly ever does.
He will break your heart, or you his, I'm sure.
If nothing else, by dying. I could weep over that.
But now it seems forced, even here in this room."

"For now, let's call a truce here on this terrace.
Later, of course, I could pick a fight on any subject
or none. There is always material for that.
But we don't come from fighting people, do we?"

"No, love will have to do, for now at least.
The heavy poems will come, have no fear.
From *temps perdu*, fertile with pain,

or perhaps from terrors far beyond this place."

"When the world rends itself, and its tainted waters
rise in the east to erode our safety here, you'll cheer.
Much as I want to discuss a lifetime of grief and craft,
talking to you, I can share this drama: I believe in karma."

Countervailing Cues

Invictus

BY WILLIAM ERNEST HENLEY

Out of the night that covers me,
black as the pit from pole to pole,
I thank whatever gods may be
for my unconquerable soul.

In the fell clutch of circumstance
I have not winced nor cried aloud.
Under the bludgeonings of chance
My head is bloody, but unbowed

Beyond this place of wrath and tears
Looms but the Horror of the shade,
And yet the menace of the years
Finds and shall find me unafraid.

It matters not how strait the gate,
How charged with punishments the scroll,
I am the master of my fate,
I am the captain of my soul.

A Reply

What a fucked-up mess that was. We couldn't get out of that firefight fast enough. And what for? To make up for
the fucked-up mess we had last night?

Was this payback/reprisal or what? Was it someone's curse?

Or was it the wet dream of that 90-day wonder who couldn't find his dick in the daylight?

He said we perform thaumaturge here—whatever that is—and he is the person who helps conjure it up.
All we have to do is soldier on and die.

Drafted soldiers all, red-eyed/weary/fear-struck/bloodied, we serve our buddies first, then us, then our country.
Who we don't serve are the bastards in charge.

Please don't think us weak. We are just scared, damaged,
afraid of dying, walking through a horror movie.
Maggots look up, patient and hungrily.

Please don't take me. Please, please, please, please, please!

We are only soldiers, on a battlefield, miles from our homes. We are not those who care what the battle is about. Those who do will not die, win or lose.

There is no awe and honor here, only desperate men waiting to see who will lose limbs, or their lives. Spare us the gallant words. Instead, return us to those we love.

Some say this will only end when all flags come down, when everyone is a brother, when all guns are banned. But isn't that the decision of those who want war?

Mindi

How do you explain death to a dog?
I can't, and that's why I didn't take Mindi to your funeral.
Instead, here she is at your gravestone.

She didn't know what we were doing here,
then somehow sensed that you were six feet under,
and tried to dig you up with tears in her eyes.

Your last words to her were, "I'm just too tired."
You said that often during the last few weeks.
Too tired to walk her, play with her, and be with her.

I wish you were here to see how much she loves you.
To remind you of what real unconditional love is,
without judgment or fault, pure, pristine, unrestrained.

I didn't show you such love, though I wished I had,
deeply, but couldn't. Mindi is here to demonstrate

how much I really loved you but just couldn't show it.

Thoughts At Dawn

It is 5:59 AM

Did I sleep at all? I'm so obsessed with him that I can't tell if I was or not. I meet someone like Joe, and I lose myself in him completely.

Now it's 6:16 AM

I tried to get at least some sleep but couldn't. His face kept appearing, zooming to me. I want him . . . now!

Later at 6:22 AM

I don't see his face anymore but his body. It is not perfectly structured and muscled. Instead, it is smooth. I want to feel it, stroke it, devour it.

Now it's 6:34 AM

Is he thinking of me? I hope so. With all my heart, I hope he is.

At 6:50 AM

I tried again to get some sleep. It was still not possible. He kept interfering. He's mesmerizing. Does he know that?

It’s 7:03 AM

My alarm went off, and I pushed the snooze button. But I couldn’t snooze. I can’t even do that.

It’s 7:10 AM

He’s like a song I can’t stop thinking about, a siren going off in my head, a favorite dessert that dares me to break my diet.

It’s 7:11 AM

My heart feels so full, so overcome with emotion that it might burst.

It’s 7:12 AM

He is so right for me in so many ways. I made a list and checked each item off. Perfection!

It’s 7:13 AM

Am I right for him? Does he have his own list? Has he checked off what is important to him?

It’s 7:14 AM

I feel so hungry for love, what I crave in love, what I need in love, and what I have not yet found in love.

It’s 7:15 AM

My heart yearns to find love, to feel love, to be in love.

It’s 7:16 AM

Love that makes my heart spin and does cartwheels, summons butterflies, and dances with them.

It's 7:17 AM

Love that has never felt like this before. Love that I have waited for. Love that endures.

It's 7:18 AM

There is so much love building in my heart now. Has it been waiting to get out? Was it always there?

It's 7:19 AM

Will all my love smother him, scare him, make him vanish? It might because it scares me.

It's 7:20 AM

I am afraid now. My love is bottomless for him, so colossal, so high, so embracing. It may be too much.

It's 7:21 AM

I have already engraved my initials on him, along the rib bone beneath his heart.

It's 7:22 AM

I stake my claim. He is mine.

On This Day

I walk and the sidewalk bends toward me,
curls to meet my feet,
and softens as feathers on a dove.

It happens when I think of you, my prince,
and I go there again to memories dark,
but also filled with love for you.

It was July 24, on a day like this, when you were born.
The heavens sent me you, and then took you back, too
quickly, so suddenly, that I had only minutes with you.

Your face was so innocent, your breath so sweet,
and you looked like an angel, before you became one.
Is that what you were always meant to be?

Then you cried, loud, for all the world to hear.
Did you cry for yourself or for me, my prince?
Can you ever forgive me, my prince, for crying too.

Instead I should have celebrated you, rejoiced you.
That is why I pick this sidewalk yearly. Here I find flowers
to place at your grave, my love, my angel, and my prince.

Tiny Perfume Bottles

My Grandmother had a collection
of tiny glass bottles, the kind for perfume,
and seemed to add to it each month.
She arranged the collection in the sun
on the sill of a window partway up the back stairs.

She'd pass them twice every day, plodding,
painfully down from her room in the morning,
one hand on the banister, one on her cane,
its tip counting the steps, and then, in the evening,
slowly and heavily, climbing back to her bed.

She rented that shadowy house, so little
light or color in it anywhere, the furnishings
all grays and browns, with somber rugs
and the black horsehair settee upon which
my grandfather had laid down to rest and had died.

But those bottles brightened that place on the staircase
with pale pinks and blues, gay yellows and greens, their
crystal stoppers sparkling, and though much had been taken from
her, she had this, a moment at the window twice each day when
she'd pause and sometimes lift a bottle to the light. Then, smiling,
she continued regally up the stairs.

Six Six Word Stories

Three words never spoken, always regretted.

Time stood still, but I didn't.

Met her, wed her, regret her.

War finally ended, and ended me.

Room for rent: apply after funeral

A young soldier, grew much older

I went, parents got folded flag.

The Snap of the Branch

Should I have an opinion about the kindling snap the branch on the family tree makes when it's broken and the ridiculous echo?

There's nothing special about being broken. Where I'm from, it's all plaster casts, walkers, and breathing machines. Bud's been dead for years, and Shirley's still blaming him for her emphysema. (I changed chronic obstructive pulmonary disease to emphysema to streamline, but Bud's real, and Aunt Shirley's real.)

I witnessed their big-eared teenage son in his coffin. He overdosed, but Shirley thinks he was murdered. This is what happens with sentences. They lead you to the edge of the powder-blue coffin that holds the corpse of a boy who loved the Dave Clark Five, and suddenly you've got a murder mystery on your hands. (The coffin wasn't actually powder-blue, but it should have been, the color of a high school prom tuxedo.)

We went to prom together before he died. I don't think I knew you weren't supposed to date your cousin. I wasn't supposed to date my cousin. Someone made the dress but not my mother. My mother didn't sew. In fact, people used to refer to her as "sir." "What can I get you, sir?" the kid at the hot-dog stand said. "You want chili sauce on that, sir?" And my father, right before he died, looked nine months pregnant. (I might as well divulge that there was no prom. No prom, no dress. Not that I wasn't asked. I was asked, but not by anyone I wanted to go with.)

My sister went to the prom all four years of high school. All of them were with someone she wanted to go with. The home-ec teacher, a family friend, made her dresses. The first one was turquoise, covered in white lace. The second, white dotted swiss with orange accent flowers. The third was the color of churned butter. The fourth, a pale pink, and she used it two years later for a wedding gown.

She married her prom date, but only after a brief dalliance with a short, charming X-ray tech with a huge mustache, who snuck into the back bedroom of the house trailer we lived in that summer and tried to kiss me. I was fourteen.

"Don't do that to my sister," I said, which was another way of saying don't do that to me, which was another way of saying don't do that to my sister.

I once wore a used prom dress, sliced in half horizontally with pinking shears, for a fourth-grade pageant when I was selected to sing "My Old Kentucky Home" wearing a stiff petticoat under a lime-green gown and twirling an orange umbrella, which my teacher called a parasol. " 'Tis summer," I sang. "The darkies are gay." (I was the worst kind of racist, the kind who can plead innocence, just nine years old and not a clue as to what darkies were.)

The teacher fed me the lyrics, and I sang in an off-key soprano, flattered to have been chosen for the job. Thus began my career as a member of the lynch mob, a simpering little white girl whose family, by then, was subsisting on cans of charity pork and beans.

Some in that town believed my mother was mixed race and treated her as such, my father a hidden Jew, his father a Hitler look-alike, his mother a Jehovah's Witness, his grandmother a kleptomaniac who stole carrot peelers and crucifixes and sewed them into her mattress, his brother a major drug dealer masking as a furniture salesman, his sister selling Avon and slowly developing emphysema while Bud smoked, hooked up to a deep-green oxygen tank and thinking back wistfully on his murdered son, and still, he made it to our house sometimes in the middle of the night, pounding on the door and moaning my mother's name.

He was a tiny man, but I always pictured him as one of those bears which is really a man, or a man who is really a bear, or a body that breaks out of the coffin and finds its way home, roaring at the door to be let in. (Is any of this true? I can't tell now since I lie so much that I have difficulty remembering what is a lie and what isn't. And that's the truth . . . Or is it?)

Playing Beethoven At The Beach

She came to me as a melody,
by Beethoven or the like,
while the sea shouted close by.

Her body so close I could sense her thoughts,
by the rise and fall of her smile,
or the slight movement of her deepest cells.

The beach was all eyes and ears and waves
dancing her, romancing her in its sway.
As last night, the moon reflected her light.

When the rhythm of the water and wave
had been overcome by the moon's pull,
she asked if I was nervous, as if I ever could.

Then she spread herself along my surface;

She seeped into my skin, and was consumed.
The only parts left were melody and mood.

Tulum

Tulum (Spanish pronunciation: [tu'lum], Yucatec Maya: *Tulu'um*) is the site of a pre-Columbian Mayan walled city which served as a major port for Coba, in the Mexican state of Quintana Roo.[1] The ruins are situated on 12-meter-tall (39 ft) cliffs along the east coast of the Yucatán Peninsula on the Caribbean Sea.[1] Tulum was one of the last cities built and inhabited by the Maya; it was at its height between the 13th and 15th centuries and managed to survive about 70 years after the Spanish began occupying Mexico. By the end of the 16th century, the site was abandoned. One of the best-preserved coastal Maya sites, Tulum is today a popular site for tourists. Some historians say mass murders occurred here, of captives of other tribes, and the sickly among the natives. And that the place is cursed by those who died grisly deaths.

According to the tourist guide (or is he a storyteller?), the red-painted war clubs are just for show. It wasn't dried blood on them.

The courage and determination of warriors who hunted jaguars in the jungle was real.

What is not real is the number of members of other tribes enslaved as workers.

What is not real is the number of captured warriors who were decapitated and torn into practical fare for the livestock.

Or fallen comrades, mortally wounded, or too sick now and no longer of value.

We'll never know the genesis of people killed, captured, and sold, so why question the narrative?

The Place of Torments? That is just a name and bears no relation to what went on there.

The tally marks on the stone of people captured, sold, and killed? That is also just speculation, spurious, and a lie.

And it is madness to believe the rumors, the lies of possible retribution. Score-settling? What is that?

Is that what you hear and read about the deaths of those who tread here?

How many tourists have fallen ill, lost fortunes, or died after visiting here?

That many you say?

Is evil-doing cumulative?

Are the wicked to be punished?

Walk on and do not think negatively.

And do not turn back if you feel it behind you.

The Darkness

It's all about waiting right now as the darkness closes in.
Death came to my father first, then my oldest brother.
Both of them within months. Both by heart attacks.

My mother followed, and, in short order, my uncle and aunt. All within weeks. Was that luck? Or was it by divine grace. They were close. Maybe they felt it right to go then.

A pause. Then my sister came next, my sweet loving sister. Then my other brother, which was again by heart attack. Both passed in December, so no Christmas for me.

I feel death stalking me, cowering me now, the last to go.
He tore through my family with ease, if you please.
And will no doubt tear through to get me.

But I am strong and I have a powerful gun.
Is that enough? Or is that just a bluff?
Or should I not care anymore?

It's a rotten life anyway isn't it?
Especially since I know,
I am the last to go.

Spared

It seems a blessing to me now that my older brother came first, then another brother, then my sister, and then me. Maybe my father was too old and tired when I came. My brother Charlie got the worst of it. Then Al. My sister wasn't spared. It was different for her, but just as cruel. And it was hard to escape the sounds of it in a four room house, crammed in like sardines, which I hated. "Keep close to the floor, or under the table," my sister would say, and she was right. And keep quiet as mouse. I did and I was spared —most of the time.

A Bird Made That Plain

The dog had been beaten
and I knew who did it.
So did the whimpering dog.

The dog had flies crawling on it,
excited, on the beat marks,
and on tears falling from its face.

He held still in the sun-blazed yard,
while I stood at the wire fence,
Trying not to cry too.

He was aware of me I think,
but he did not turn—
except his eye, slightly.

What was he waiting for?
Was he listening for a return of the strap?
I would wait there with him.

Maybe if we both were standing guard
There would be no second time.
A bird made that plain with its cry.

I Want To Remember Summer This Way

All that simmers on the stove is holy.
That is what my mother would say.

But she said it in Italian,
which sounds more meaningful and true.

All afternoon her pots would work
filled to the brim with her art, with her passion.

Ours now are not as busy, nor as holy.
Still, the beans and tomatoes and squash
surrender their juices, their tender morsels
plump and swell with delight.

In the yard, we plant rhubarb, cauliflower,
and artichokes; potatoes, carrots, ginger,
cupping wet earth over tubers, our labor
the germ of later sustenance and renewal.

Across the field, the sound of a baby crying
as we carry in the last carrots,
whorls of butter lettuce gone wild,
and a prize of young fingerling potatoes.

I want to remember this day—
late September, sun streaming through

the window, bread loaves, and golden
bunches of grapes on the table.

From the first crunch of lettuce,
through spoonfuls of hot soup that bites,
our lips, smiling, filling us,
with what we have blessed ourselves.

An Anniversary

Amid fountains of floral that didn't look real,
she shimmered in a gown too precious to be used twice,
among relatives and friends, and cats that ate the canary.

With chaperones of asphodel from the depths of her soul,
She winked and sashayed the aisle, pledging
between competing saints, a virtuous life.

As from the heavens above, actually the balcony,
violins and voices filled the church with sounds
so kinfolk could weep harmoniously.

I will be aurora to your borealis, she said.
And I will be your tower of strength, he said.
Then they wed, and didn't, though they did remember.

A Temptress

She was a temptress in red, roaming the night scenes,
wicked and evil inside, blond and blue-eyed on the out,
the stuff of dreams, or more often night screams.

She saw him there, looking tall and debonaire,
a prize to be won, her goal, her delight,
on another blood-draining terror-filled night.

But he was with someone, and she quickly remedied that.
A few words caused a spat, which left him all alone.
Was he a afraid, a little unsure? She didn't have a clue.

They went for a walk, and he talked quite a lot,
filling her with words that she hadn't heard before,
causing her plans, and much more, to be abused and sore.

Then suddenly he vanished, leaving her famished.
Sometimes you can't trust those you meet at night,
and a predator may meet another predator's acolyte.

Fabled Pot Of Gold

If only I owned the fabled pot of gold,
or an assortment of gems from the earth,
diamonds and emeralds, rubies and Sapphires,
I would spread them before you; give all my worth.

Had I the rights to nature's best views,
majestic mountains, to seascapes with spray,
I'd wrap them with tissues, box them with bows,
And to you my love, I would gladly gift them all away.

Everything the heavens have in the skies,
the sun, moon and planets—all that's on high,
both in the daytime, and in the darkest of nights,
they would be yours, conveyed with nary an outcry.

Best yet are my dreams, alas I am poor,
but they are true treasures far more than gold,
I will spread them around you, to dazzle you blind,
They're everything I have; my wishes, my future untold.

I Struck The Match

I am a survivor. This much I know.
Daily. It's the living that gives
me trouble. Not the life.

Take my failures as a son. Or not.
They unlock doors
I'd rather be left closed,

I speak in tongues, track the life
like so much mud.
No beast of the earth, instead a bird.

A desperate winged thing—
a bat, a bird, or a butterfly.
That is the appeal.

My independence. Now pinned.
No need to spare my feelings.

Nor make sounds I know.

The net you cast was meant for me.
What ensnared, even knowing
how this story's meant to end.

You fell for me anyway.
Gnawed your paw off in the trap.
The trap meant for me.

The two of us creatures
patched with cruelty, born of blood,
or red clay. Which we deserve.

I find I love you too late.
Your desire a cheap prize
to die for. Or to live for.

I bid thee welcome.
Will join your journey and your fate.
When you burn, I struck the match.

Impersonal

At ten, I learned to write a love letter
to be put away, to seduce a different day.

Love, then, was a soft pencil script
or, if I dared, a dark impersonal font.

Imagining in words a future that
can only be imagined in perfect ways.

A future that can be altered by a word, a line.
Many a night falling asleep with ideal love.

How the crypto-siren song could spark
a conversation between the sheets.

All drawn certain. All the while uncertain.
I watched the scenes appear.

Then strange, unpredictable turns came.
Compelling me to learn.

Compelling me to return. To everything.
Showing me, eventually, nothing.

Status quo, acquaintances, the past,
neglected at the bottom of the list.

Sometimes a convention evaporated
before my eyes—after I knew it.

Was it all just chance? Nothing fate?
But I persisted, willful and cross.

About what could only be confessed
to my loving heart, or to a blank screen.

I cringed to hear the door slam,
scanning to see if life belonged.

Was it crushed? Deleted? Delivered?
Or simply disappeared.

Astonish And Decay

Life exists. You exist. Nothing has happened, though everything might still. All the unknowns exist in the ether, like dark matter, fulfilling some balance and weight. These bright, unfocused days are full of the kind of pleasure that is boredom drawn from belonging.

We scanned the pond for fish, hoping one would see us and flip to say hello. It was possible; everything was possible, even the most unrealistic. Later, the probable made us think differently. Life's intuited demands, performances of fear moved by the real thing.

Rhapsodies of gossip and long hair, we wanted who we wanted for as long as we wanted them, then pity, then farewell. Disappointment made you otherworldly, opening inside you, filling as it holed, then suddenly relieved with ordinary gentleness, permitting you to laugh.

Eyes dulled from the ether's chlorine, and all edges glowed. Oh, to be so peopled and present, even anguish tempted to rejoice in feeling, even the splinter as it settled into the skin. Summer, yielding like laughter into silence. The secret of youth is how it keeps on going.

And it does. It goes on and on, lifetimes in one day—eons in a week. While you digest history and syntax, a more significant part is still playing chords on a guitar, mastering "Blackbird" with sincere piety, awake for all the ways tomorrow might astonish and lead to decay.

Butterflies

Butterflies, by example, illustrate life.
Seasons change, and they do,

slowly, miraculously, by nature and fortune,
by rapture and miracle.

Of course, they are a metaphor to make more of us.
From one thing to be another,

and another all our own; a kingdom swelled
to endless summer and semblance.

Your eyes echoed in your hands, reflected warmly on me.
Something happened to the leaves

to make you leave. Then, by example, the changing
changed. The changing ceased.

We grew away, and language followed.
Married now, you are gently

redacted. What's left, a looking back,
a ghostly shell on the beach, more light

than object, faith than fact.
The butterfly knows to outgrow

but keep dear, sure of becoming
beyond itself. No color can

explain them. And how, not seeing,
we have known them all along.

Of What To Come

Along the dirt road leading to my grandmother's house,
women would light candles at dusk. At least then. All in unison as if someone rang a bell, and somebody always might.

The almanac would tell them what time they needed light, when the moon waned and the night grew dark enough to see all the stars; when it was ghost time, and also weather.

I almost see her at her parish church, on the same road, at dusk and snow falling, while inside the candles guttering, a head nodding so the quiet ones can talk. A bell; another.

Or say this is possible: a childhood kitchen, a tongue worn smooth on the spoon's belly. A more precise form of life, of living, divining, dying, and all to chance instead of fate.

A storyline breaks to threads, until the last, the one a child will save for later when it gets dark: a face suddenly open to all the winds, to all of what will come, or nothing.

A Primer For The Four Horsemen of the Apocalypse

When all the horsemen show up late, and no one seems to be in proper costume, one has to resort to the accouterments of elegy, if not schoolboy lessons. For I, the lamb of God/the lion of Judah, have to summon these at the proper time and in the appropriate way. Are they even in the right colors? On the suitable horses?

First is Conquest, in white, strolling around a white horse, not sitting nor astride. What's up with that? He carries a bow but no string and no arrows. What's up with that twice? Would that invoke pestilence? Christ or Antichrist?

Next is War, in red, without sword or shield, but says he is Civil Strife now, or possibly Conflict, and can't make up his mind. I tell him he must. And he is to stop the wordplay. War is hell. Nothing else will do.

The third is a horseman in black, thin as a rail. Good. Symbolizing Famine, of course. Or Plague. But where are the scales? He must have scales. Why? Because with them, he can dole out without restraint and mercy that which results in the absence of bread or beasts of the earth.

Last is the final horseman, Death, who escaped from hell he looks and kills with a sword in war or civil strife, plague, or famine. (Get that first horseman?) Dead is dead, no matter the niceties of death or how it came about. And he needs the others. They are a team. Does he know that?

I take Death aside, help dress him as a pilgrim, despite his protests, and place him left of center—the side of the road—where he engages with poor saps who believe there is no arguing with Death.

Me? I know better. But I must remain faithful to the customs and etiquettes of my position and yield to my only purpose of the elegy—an inborn fear of death and a holy reverence for the communiqué.

So delicate Death I prop with baskets of toes and teeth, testicles and tongue, and have done so with a song that has always been my curse, and I wonder what will Death the critic write about the chorus in the morning's edition.

I wonder how hard it is to find a romantic nickelodeon these days because they are all obsessed with death and who knew that when we rehearsed our lines about his love of potatoes, cleaned and shaven, pocketfuls dancing in the arms of a black pot, we would all agree this sounded trite, yet, if not through food how else convince an audience of the imminent resurrection in act four?

Conquest howls for direction, so I take him by the sleeve and remind him how the hero was nearly lost to nineteen-forty-four, to the red sand of Normandy, and then how, like Lazarus, he rose from the darkest night to daylight, dirty eared and unshaven, and brought a message we could not abide because he was still only a man in a man's shape.

Conquest needs a hero, and there are none anymore.

War and Famine? They will follow anyone and no one. But they ride with Conquest and Death.

The Nature Of Things

Curiosity opened my eyes.

Hurt and damage closed them.

Trust opened my heart.

Betrayal and treachery closed it.

Generosity opened my spirit.

Ingratitude closed it.

Expectation opened my mind.

Disappointment closed it.

Perfection in anything is but a dream

that reality will eventually crush.

A Recipe For Stew

It is a painting in a museum, but it is also
someone's shopping list for a hearty stew
constructed many hundreds of years ago.

It may be too big to serve as a recipe card,
but it is that anyway, plainly and clearly.
You just need a guide to see all it shows,
and what to take from its pastoral scene:

The snow is white, as potatoes and onions
brought cold from a cellar and peeled are white
as well, no matter the ruddy brown covers.

It is too late in the season for carrots,
thus not one dab of that orange,
nor any tomatoes, still in the New World,
yet to be cooked within Flanders.

Whatever's available here will get dropped
into the pot with a pinch of black pepper,
like the skaters sprinkled over the pond.

Everyone's starved in this mountainside village,
the three bent disappointed hunters,
twelve drooling dogs at their heels,
the four aproned women feeding sticks to a fire
in the background, and the frozen slope now suddenly fragrant
with the dream of rabbit,

of chewy legs bubbling for hours in a kettle.

But that rabbit, so clever, was not snared,
and the hunters, embarrassed, afraid to go home,
stomp downhill dejected, their long sharp sticks
on their shoulders, useless now and so heavy.

The three motionless birds perched in the trees
are awaiting the scraps and will wait and wait.
The one other bird, a magpie or shrike
just now flying away, is more clever and knows
to depart.

But just in case, he turns slightly, slowly around
on the tip of a wing, to come gliding back
into the frame, but this when we're no longer
finding so much in the picture and have set it aside.
The bird will wing in for the succulent stew bones
that ought to be found in the snow.

On Selfishness

Being self-centered is hard,
it is so very, very hard indeed,
and against what you were taught,
about self-sacrifice, generosity, and love.
And about greed, meanness and being ingrate.

But be self-centered,
make it all about you first.
Do it to be happy, contended,
powerful, strong, healthy, carefree,
Instead of feeling guilt, loathing, grumpy.

Choose yourself.
It will be hard of course,
but worth it in the long run.
The hardest thing you'll ever do?
Perhaps. But worth it for the best you.

Seeking Someone

When I seek a lover, I look for how he may care for love. Does he hold it as a precious thing? To be cherished? To be prized? To be carried on high, guarded, but shown for all the world to see? That's the way he is to treat me.

I seek no physical requirements of a man. No structure of body or face, no voice or refined style, no courtesies of court. No, I look for patience that will allow me time to either come to him as I wish, or for him to wait for hours for me.

Is he caring? Is he gentle? Is he willing to give me a sense of purpose, a road of my own? I am a mass of deep complexity. Does he have the ability, the flexibility, the attitude that will defer time and place to me? As I will to he.

Does he have an open heart? Can he dream? Can he see beyond the norm? Will he see that I am heading toward passageways that are not now known? And can his heart blend his dreams, visions, desires into mine? As I do to thee.

Lessons

My first lesson about love
taught me everything,
until love ended.

After my second lesson about love
I knew all there was to know
until that ended too.

Those were the lessons about love.
I thought I knew until I didn't.
About loving until I didn't.

Lies and Truths

I lied to him and to myself; yes, I admit it.

Why?

I lied to him
and to myself
perhaps because
no matter how
many times
I said my love had died,
that I had killed it,
it would never die,
nor be any different
from (roaming
loose among the lies
I also told all year, inside
my heart, and memory, and
future imaginings) the time
I said I didn't dent the car.

I had, of course, but I guess
that would be a felony as well.

In truth, I didn't lie to him; no, I didn't.

How?

I told the truth

to him and to myself
about my emotions,
my feelings, my desires.
My love of him
is not the same
because things change
and we change with them
and what we felt before
is no more; what it was
is no more, is gone,
into memories,
where they cannot
ever be again the same
because the one I loved is gone.

I don't love him the same way, of course,
and that is another felony as well.

Greed

At last I thought I could get everything
I wanted.
Then I realized that everything I needed
I already had.

Different

When you become beautiful, they treat you differently.
Their eyes open as never before and become darts of attention focused as laser beams on you.

In school hallways, in classrooms, in the cafeteria, gym,
and music rooms—even in the bathrooms—everywhere
and anywhere, you stand out.

They all see you differently now. Some with envy, some
with lust, and some with sheer disgust at what you have
that they do not.

You see it in their eyes. Or their lips as they quiver.
They seem friendly, but they're not. You should feel safe,
but you do not.

Suddenly everything has nuance and is weighed down
by appearance. It feels as if you are carrying something heavy on your shoulders.

Suddenly you instinctively know that you are inside their minds,
their thoughts, being considered an aberration,
like a freak of nature.

Suddenly they expect you to be comfortable with your new self, mind, and disposition in tune with your outward appearance. To answer in a new way different from before.

You think of all the days back then, when you were a puddle to be stepped over, a stain to be avoided, when their long necks crisscrossed above you, keeping themselves from you.

You had resolved back then that you would never do that. But now it's payback time and you have many scores to settle, don't you?

Even if you become a face on a magazine cover. Or many covers. Does it matter? Of course not. You can never forget. The scars won't let you.

What is Life?

Life is to be lived,
to be lived with urgency,
with adventure, with vigor,
and a sense of wonder and awe.
With travel, to learn, and to expand,
and with appreciation of all things new,
different, or not realized before firsthand.
Life, it is too short to be wasted or neglected.

Life

Live a life so full and so fulfilling
that you can never have enough
time in your life to ever do it all.

A Wikipedia Account Of Me

This is an incomplete summary of my life,
my happiest moment and unhappiest,
that I choose to post to the world.

The first entry is the date of birth: 1/1/2000.
How that happened is a mystery to me,
and is even greater to my parents.

The second is a special moment when I was ten,
walking, a dollar in my hand for ice cream,
and thinking nothing could be better.

I lived in a magical world then, where all was fun,
everything was free, and nothing hurt me.
Life was as perfect as life could be.

There is an illustration of this perfect moment.
The word Utopia is below it, and it shows
the smiling eyes and smiling face of me.

It could have been a picture of a newborn infant
held in the cradling arms of a loving mother,
and be one and the same as that of me.

Where does one go then after absolute perfection?
The broad arc must lie south and downward to
the opposite, the worse that could ever be.

Do you need an illustration to show such a horror?
Even that could not be as convincing as it was.
Because it was far too much for me to bear.

That was now a year ago, and oddly enough, 1/1/2022.
Was that fate or the nature of contrasting forces?
Or perhaps it was countervailing equilibrium.

Did the author of my life stay up nights to get it right?
Including his research, days compiling, collating,
and the absolute worst superlatives imaginable.

Does this entry have a point? Something to be shared?
It does, of course. It's a fable and has wisdom in it.
Life is a pendulum that will eventually balance.

Waiting

I wait for the love of my life
who has not found me . . . yet.

I keep my fires burning inside me,
waiting of thee with all my emotions,
all my love in check, building, staying.

When he comes—and he surely will—
Oh my, how my love will encircle him,
astonish him with so much love for him.

Will he have waited for me the same way?
With all his love embedded deep inside him?
I truly trust that is so. He is on his way, I know.

A Light

There was a mist of darkness, gloom, despair,
and then you were there.

Through all the darkness surrounding me,
you came to let light be.

Craving You

The way you say my name
tends to drive me insane.
The formation of your lips
is a personal lettered kiss.

Your voice so soft, so sweet,
a melody, and it must repeat.
What kind of malady is this?
Not a virus, but shear bliss.

A Day

Will there be a day when you stop searching? When you won't look in strangers' eyes for what you're looking for.

Haven't you had enough cold times, cold beds, with nothing but cold thoughts that cannot warm you?

One day you will find the person meant for you, who eases the pain in your heart, who knows why you are you.

Why didn't those other relations work? Why did you go from one heartache to another, over and over again?

Maybe one must go through so many headaches to appreciate what is meant to be in happiness and fulfillment.

Some day you will look into the eyes of one person and feel what no other person has made you feel—true love.

You will look into that person's eyes and realize they are the only eyes you want to look at for the rest of your life.

That ended for me when I met you. Now it's up to you to see me the way I have seen you—my perfect person!

Feelings

You make me feel alive
and dangerous to touch
and somehow radioactive.

You dismiss the voice
in my head that says *Stop*
and replace it with a loud *Go*.

You make every day such fun,
exciting, thrilling, invigorating.
You make my feelings come alive.

Inward And Back

I had walked the earth barely knowing myself
or where I was going, not knowing what I felt
or why, and unable to see what was true
and what was false.

I worked hard to repress experiences and observations instead of
letting them teach me. Instead of facing
situations head-on, I ran from them, and fear resulted,
then pain, then anger, and finally self-loathing.

When I finally faced my problems, I became free.

I was free to learn by observing, accepting, and responding appropriately, with honesty and without judgment. That released me from the tension that had always been in my mind and surrounding my heart.

The keys to my freedom were in the darkness. I went there with the light of awareness and returned knowledgeable and acutely aware. My experiences bring wisdom, not fear nor loathing, to my mind and heart.

On The Nature Of Change

In many people's eyes
change is a fault or crime.
Even though you try to improve,
they will condemn you for being different.

So you can't go home,
not anymore if you're different.
and will drift on the wind of chance—
wherever you land you will be as an outsider.

Then accept your role,
that of a wanderer, a nomad.
At least you can stand alone finally.
And become one who lives and dies on their own.

You must learn to be you,
content to inhabit your own space—
any news from far away can no longer disturb you.
Turn your back on the past: let it vanish from your mind.

Another Day

Pushing away from her bed
with her body still tired
even after seven hours,
she lifts her head awkwardly,
not daring to see herself
in the mirror opposite her bed just now—
hair all a mess,
with eyes, skin, and face showing
what neglect and age
has done to make her pay.

She groans,
and sends a silent prayer upward
toward a God, any god
still listening to help her
get through another day.

Her scuffed slippers are comfortable,
and the water feels good
splashed against her face.
She kicks at the air as she turns
at the old dog of inertia
that would rather stay in bed.
It growls, then shrinks out of the way.

His Concert

Today, on a commuter train,
sat a sad little man of maybe sixty,
wearing a baggy black suit, a white shirt
buttoned to the neck, no tie, but with cufflinks.

He had thinning silver hair oiled back,
and he began singing quite softly the words
to a song that seemed from his hidden ear piece
connected to a device somewhere in his coat pocket.

His voice was shrill, very high-pitched
and seemed to reach heights only dogs hear.
Some thought it fine. Others as me craved silence.
When he ended I felt sad as if I had ended his concert.

At A Parade

I could hear the parade three blocks before it arrived at our spot on the curb. Leading the way was a high school band—our high school band, the Wilson High School Mighty Mules—and don't ask how it got its name, which is dumb I know, but it's the best thing about the parade.

The band played a Sousa march that sounded loud even from a distance, with trombones, trumpets, and tubas blaring out and drums thundering, booming across the sky. Occasional high-pitched sounds of piccolos came flying in, barging in as if they were stowaways, not part of the band.

The music grew louder as the band marched toward us, bobbing in waves like light on choppy water, becoming louder and louder still, with arms flaring to make those sounds and girls in tights stomping on naked legs in boots with flippy tassels and tossing batons skyward.

But before the band was the ceremonial head, a convertible with two soldiers sitting, waving at the crowd, each almost too old even to do that much. Dressed in uniforms that didn't fit anymore, one too tight and the other too large, they sat at opposite ends, dividing the crowd between them.

The convertible is holding a white gold-bordered banner, frayed now, like the soldiers, on which is printed "Our Greats From The Greatest Generation." It is not cared for between appearances, just like the soldiers. Are they from World War II? Certainly not Vietnam, the Iraq War, or even the Gulf War.

The Korean War? No, that was just a "police action."

The Afghanistan War? Don't make me laugh.

Once we had soldiers from The Great War, which became World War I after an even greater war reduced it to a minor war at second thought.

And does anyone still remember soldiers from the Spanish-American War? Or the Civil War? Didn't they live pretty long too?

The ones I remember best were from the Spanish-American War. Yes, I am old, maybe that's why I remember them best. The last three of them (or was it four?) were in the parade in 1985. Still alive somehow and almost forgotten, they were phlegmy old men in ancient uniforms.

In 1985? Yes. Still alive then, they seemed to lean forward into the light of the future, spectacles glinting, on their way to their graves in short order, which they would reach within months. Taps for them was all they had to look forward to, a ceremonial sendoff, the pops of five old rifles, and then ....

A Message To The Moon

The moon on cold nights seems to shiver,
as do the trees over crusted snow.
This night I watched the oak outside my window
prepare itself, brace itself for the long frosty vigil
before dawn freed it from the icy grip of the cold.

All night the moon was a lamp held steady
over the oak, befriending it, companioning it.
You could almost see the tree giving thanks,
by a shiver, by a quiver—or was it the wind?
Would that be enough? Was something more needed?

That was when the tree composed a long letter,
thoughtfully forming each word in the copperplate script of its shadows. From a window on the stairs, I watched it work, the pale-blue stationery appropriate and waiting to be filled with the sentiments coming so slowly that I grew impatient and climbed up to my bed to rest.

I fell asleep wondering to whom the tree might give its writing. Have astronauts started going back to the moon? And why? The moon is a bleak place beyond its coldness. It was right to give it up as a place to visit. Better to go to Mars, Venus, or anywhere else more hospitable.

When I awoke, the sky was gray and cold, the sun hidden in clouds, and the tree was just standing there, reaching up into a few scattered snowflakes then beginning to fall, not trying to catch them but letting them slip through its branches, and the letter, whatever its message, was gone.

Priorities

They never call to say

Nothing has changed, though it seldom does, except that everyone gets a day, then a week, a month and a year older.

They never call to say

I hope you are better, though that is your main focus now, and everything else is rendered simply secondary.

They never call to say

You need wakening, though that's what they think as they wrap themselves around trees and enjoy the feel of bark.

They never call to say

We didn't want you to dream, though that's what they expect when they show you utopia and promise to take you there.

The Task Of A Fool

There was talk of it being a friendship at first.
People say those things when they break up,
when they once had much more between them.
Were they lies? Or simply wishes?

We are at our very cores emotional beings,
and the memories of our bodies linger on
well after our minds have forgot such things.
Can our bodies ever be just friends now?

What once attracted us—the beauty, the charm—
it is still there and does not disappear.
Nor does it hide. Our eyes still see it, sense it,
and we want to converge with it all again.

No talk will fulfill, no exchange of greetings will still,
all those feelings that emerge when you meet.
They are wild and cannot be tamed by societal grace.
They will escape and tear all the barriers down again.

So try, if you will, to go against your nature,
and talk in tongues with someone who was a lover.
That is the task of a fool, and you'll realize it when
your babble renders you crazy and you kneel at his feet.

A Hymn To Him

His home is on a hill overlooking a valley, and everything
else his life has granted or has enchanted him. Can he ask for more? He does, daily, weekly, and monthly, as much as he can, as much as he can imagine.

His room is quiet, but for the rustle of the blanket under which
he's slept burrowed deep in the best nesting sense,
that wholesome dark down there, where he lay on a field
of old summers, on a gone-to-seed garden.

His thoughts are fettered, yet chained and in the grip; he won't let himself think and sits hiked up now, naked to the waist, like a stone in the bedclothes, his mind festooned on the angle of incidence his life is taking, the robust weariness he feels.

The scene, the bright proscenium outside his windows
shows a warming trend has begun, a white shock of blue
corrupting the snow in the furrows, the avenues between
rows of harvested grain transformed into clots of slush, as if some flaw has given way in his flesh.

His possessions, chosen and accreted, piled in various
corners of the room, identify him, like the signature at
the bottom of a painting. The room haunts itself morbidly forward toward others, in turn disintegrating, a procession whose personal connectedness, no matter how many times learned, is no use to him.

He prays with the intensity of an iconoclast, his throat made raw by the effort, face flushed warm like a child who's been crying, prays to the God of eternal, of the speculative, and the starving, the damaged tribes; of cheap trinkets and elisions; to the God of unruly stones in the olive light; to the God who wields the broom of time that sweeps away mountains, filling the rivers with their fragments.

Behold, God eats the grass, and the meadows are trampled; metamorphoses and is color. All colors evaporate. No more the book of pages, the rustle of quartz. There is sound but no uses.

The centrifuge sucks in, and the sigh goes unheeded; only now and then do the serpentine shifts of the ordinary add up. But how to show it pictorially?

The sky gathers at the window an iridescence. He has earned the right not to speak. He has nobody for whom to wait. But a man's nativity has its uses, and he lingers on, light as the floss of cotton candy, the hours unmoved.

All this is a metaphor; all movement is centripetal.Within stone, the core begins to create itself, sweating tears, waking, repeating old habits, then replacing them with new ones, learned over a lifetime, of things that cannot change.

About The Author

Tanya Angel

She is an author of short stories and flash fiction. Her writings have been published online and in print by amazon.com. She has authored five collections of fiction, three books of poetry, and a novel, Impersonal, is to be published later this year.

Books By This Author

As If I Had Wings

A preteen, a young divorcee, a woman who endured a near-death experience, and one who did not, plus eight more compelling female characters fill the pages of this collection of short stories. This is from the lead story:

"I was hungry now and greedy; for everything that had been denied me in life. I wanted so much, and so fast; to be a strong woman, as well as soft and feminine; to have many friends and to be left alone; to travel and to stay home; to read good books and to write my own; to live life fully, and cut corners when it pleased me; to be selfish and to be unselfish. I saw the contradictions in my needs but cared not. You see, I wanted it all. And nothing had better stand in my way . . . even me!

Paris Street Stories

This is a collection of short fiction and poetry about life. Why are they French street stories? Voltaire once said novels were fictionalized versions of how people live their lives and short stories about how they actually live their lives. He also said most of what he learned in life was from Paris's streets, where his character was forged. And that great things happen in this world —nature's calamities, famines, and pestilence, but the real dangers people may face daily are what awaits them around the corner, what is often lurking in the blackened hearts of people we know. The most terrible wars are sometimes fought within the walls of our own homes, and sometimes people we love, the people who are supposed to love us, protect us, cause the most damage, the most pain. Living is dangerous, but it is also its own reward. We gain from such experiences because we survive them. Pain and change are always coming, but we were built to take it and be stronger as a result.

The Secret Lives Of Smiles

The Secret Lives of Smiles is a collection of heart-felt poetry twenty years in the making. It contains a mixture of observations, experiences and emotions each of us see and feel at some point of time in our life. It took quite sometime to distill them to purity and then pour them from my heart onto the printed page; Then to let the words ripen sufficiently before they were shared with the world. Some are lyrical, others measured and straightforward; still others are classic in structure. Indeed they run the gamut of style and substance. The ironic shares space with the commonplace, and the lyric ballad with ideas that are infinite. The book reflects much more than how one human feels, but how we all feel.

When The Heart Laughs It Shows And When It Doesn't It Shows Even Move

“A woman’s heart is a deep ocean of secrets.” --Gloria Stuart as the older Rose in the film Titanic.

As so brilliantly depicted in that amazing movie of love found and lost, a woman’s heart is a hidden place where love once sparked can endure and never be extinguished by the passage of time. The heart feels love and loss deeply, and has its reasons that reason cannot know.

Journey there through these stories, to the hearts of an array of women and discover their secrets -- feel what they felt, see what they saw-- and know them. A woman's heart feels things the eyes cannot see, and knows what the mind cannot understand. Discovery of them begins there.

Where The Heart Is

What is your favorite reading spot? Is it on on the beach, in the back yard, in bed or the bathtub? This is a collection of stories to take there -- to the place that is your own where you can lose yourself in a story -- no matter that sometimes your reading spot is a crowded bus or subway, or in the break-room at lunchtime.

All That Glitters

This collection of short stories are snippets of life, introducing you to characters that will take you inside their hearts and souls to help you learn a little something about yourself. Some narratives will make you laugh; some will make you cry; some will make you think differently about the wonder, awe, and mystery of life. I hope you will enjoy reading them as much as I enjoyed writing them.

www.ingramcontent.com/pod-product-compliance
Lightning Source LLC
LaVergne TN
LVHW052050160826
845678LV00015B/3155

* 9 7 9 8 3 5 2 1 7 6 0 9 2 *